SPORES FROM SHARNOTH
AND OTHER MADNESSES

Through gates of unparalleled dream, P'rea bids you a thousand welcomes.

"Excellent poetry of the weird … If you love Lovecraft and admire formal poetic form and structure then this professional debut collection must be in your collection!"
—Scott E. Green, author *Contemporary Science Fiction, Fantasy, and Horror Poetry*

"Leigh Blackmore … is a superb fantasy poet, indeed, one of the highest order."
—Michael Fantina, author *Sirens and Silver*, *This Haunted Sea*

"This remarkable little book of verse at once establishes Blackmore as one of the leading weird poets of our time, fit to be mentioned with the likes of Bruce Boston, G. Sutton Breiding, Ann K. Schwader, and others … Blackmore reveals penetrating insight into the authors to whom he pays tribute and an understanding of the metrical precision that sets them apart from the lazybones free verse that too often clutters our poetry journals."
—S. T. Joshi, author *Emperors of Dreams, The Weird Tale, I Am Providence*

"Magnifique! Sobresaliente! Mumtaaz! [Blackmore] definitely has the touch … and of course I can tell he has the same sources of inspiration as I do."
—Richard L. Tierney, author *Savage Menace, Collected Poems, The Drums of Chaos*

"Outstanding technical quality … deeply felt and well-crafted poems. The occasional inversions and older language, used with discretion, do not mar in any way these often fear-filled runes, but impart a needed and enjoyable variety … These poems, more often than not, strike home again and again."
—Donald Sidney-Fryer, author *Songs and Sonnets Atlantean, The Atlantis Fragments*

SPORES FROM SHARNOTH AND OTHER MADNESSES

Leigh Blackmore

Foreword by S. T. Joshi

Edited by Charles Lovecraft

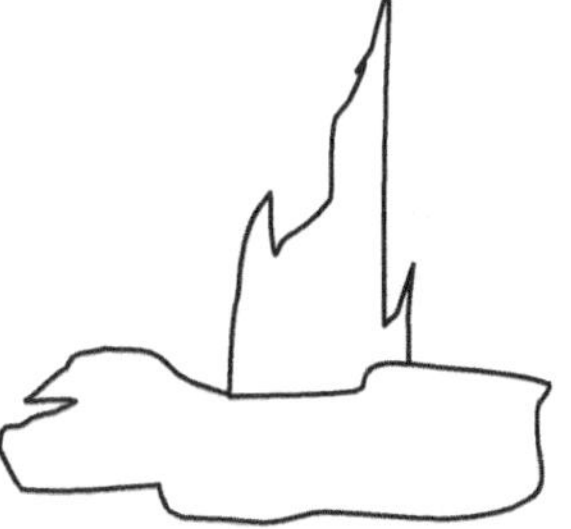

P'REA PRESS
SYDNEY, AUSTRALIA
2013

Leigh Blackmore (b. 30 June 1959), writer, editor, manuscript assessor and occultist, lives in Wollongong, Australia with his family, several cats, and way too many books. His previous publications include: *Brian Lumley: A New Bibliography*, *H. P. Lovecraft and Lovecraft Criticism: An Annotated Bibliography: Supplement 1980–1984* (with S. T. Joshi), *Terror Australis* (magazine, publisher and editor), *Terror Australis: Best Australian Horror* (anthology, editor), *Harlan Ellison/Terry Dowling/Jack Dann: A Bibliographic Checklist*, *Terry Dowling: Virtuoso of the Fantastic*, and *Cemetery Rose* (www.lulu.com "print-on-demand").

Published by P'rea Press, Sydney, Australia.

First edition September 2008. Revised reprint August 2010, May 2013, February 2016.

Book designed by David E. Schultz.
Cover created by Gavin L. O'Keefe.
Publisher's logo created by Charles Lovecraft.
Set in Goudy Old Style BT 11 point.
Printed by Lightning Source International.

National Library of Australia Cataloguing-in-Publication entry:

Author:	Blackmore, Leigh.
Title:	Spores from Sharnoth and other madnesses / Leigh Blackmore, S. T. Joshi.
Edition:	4th rev.
ISBN:	9780980462524 (pbk.)
Notes:	Includes index.
	Bibliography.
Other Authors/Contributors:	
	Joshi, S. T., 1958–
	Lovecraft, Charles, 1955– editor.
Dewey Number:	A821.4

To Margi Curtis & Graham Wykes
(the other two of the Three Musketeers!)

CONTENTS

Part II: . . . and Other Madnesses

FOREWORD

The expression of the emotions of horror, terror, fear, wonder, and awe can be found in the oldest poetry known to man. What is Homer's *Odyssey*—with its successive displays of the sorceress Circe, the seductive Sirens, the one-eyed monster Polyphemus, and the entire tableau of Odysseus's descent to the Underworld—but an array of encounters with the bizarre? The battle of Beowulf and Grendel; the nine circles of Hell in Dante; the wizard Merlin in Malory's *Morte d'Arthur:* the poetry of the West is replete with the supernatural, proceeding down through Coleridge's "Rime of the Ancient Mariner" to the work of such twentieth-century masters as Clark Ashton Smith, H. P. Lovecraft, Joseph Payne Brennan, Ann K. Schwader, and many others. But as is the case with horror literature in prose, weird verse is often dismissed as a kind of poor relation to "genuine" poetry. The poet and critic Winfield Townley Scott wrote, "To scare is a slim purpose in poetry." Maybe so— if to scare is the *only* motive the poet adopts.

But because wonder and terror are central facets of our emotional life, their expression in literature—including poetry—is for that reason not only justifiable but essential. Such expression will serve the cardinal function of giving a voice to fears that might otherwise remain nameless and undefined. Was it not Aristotle who pointed to the cathartic function of poetry and drama by means of its display of "pity and fear"?

Leigh Blackmore, in a poetic career that has spanned more than thirty years, has given shape to some of our deepest fears in this slim but substantial volume. To be sure, some of his poems are meant to recall the powerful emotions we have experienced in reading the great horror literature of the past, as in the pungent sonnets recounting various tales by Lovecraft and Arthur Machen. The manner in which Leigh has distilled the effect of an entire tale within the compact form of a sonnet is remarkable. As several other poems suggest, Leigh has also been moved by the figure of the man H. P. Lovecraft, and the poem written on 21 August 1990—at the conclusion of the Lovecraft Centennial Conference in Providence, Rhode Island, an event that encapsulated Lovecraft's emergence from pulp hackdom to the status of a major writer—is a moving tribute to the power of Lovecraft's personality.

Clark Ashton Smith—substantially superior to Lovecraft as a poet—has inspired Leigh both personally and literarily. The long poem "Memoria: A Fragment from the Book of Wyvern" has something of the density of diction and vividness of metaphor found in Smith's "The Hashish-Eater." Leigh has even made bold to attempt haiku in English, as Smith had done (not entirely successfully) in the 1940s. It is not to be denied that Leigh has mastered this most delicate and winsome of poetic forms.

There is something fitting in the inclusion of the poem "Terror Australis," whose title echoes the splendid anthology of Australian horror writing that Leigh edited in 1993; for Leigh stands at the vanguard of a remarkable renaissance of Australian weird fiction, poetry, and criticism that includes other such luminaries as Phillip A. Ellis, Charles Lovecraft, Benjamin Szumskyj, and, most recently, the transplanted American Perry M. Grayson. With this core of talent, it is likely that Australia will leave a substantial mark upon the weird literature of the present and future.

—S. T. Joshi

Moravia, New York
April 2008

Introduction

Happy with the world as it is? Not me. I have always wanted a world of romance, danger and excitement . . . that is, a world founded not in bland reality, but in poetry . . .

—Leigh Blackmore[1]

Imagination is at the centre of Leigh Blackmore's universe. It is a universe of intricate creation, located in the vague depths of a mind, place and time warp, inhabited by fantastic and horrible beings, a universe of arcane ritual, spectacular events, gorgeous perceptions, and terrifying, gruesome uncertainties.

From his youth, Blackmore has explored his creation and shared it with us in word, music, ritual, wizardry and art. From the age of fifteen years, with friends, he began publishing magazines and forming societies to "promote the study and appreciation of . . . important fantasy writers."[2] In an inspiring way, he has held to his vision of his universe through the vicissitudes of pedestrian life. He has encouraged interest in weird literature in Australia through his bibliographies, past book trade roles, editing and publishing, conference and media exposure, and networks of literary contacts. For those of us who have read his short stories and poetry, his publications are too few!

Now in mid-life, Blackmore has a body of unpublished literary work including poetry from his adolescence until the present. Poems for this collection were selected from that body of work on the basis of subject: their weird content. This is a major, but not exclusive, interest and

---

1. "Satanic Milk and Thundersun: Some Notes on Poetic Influences" (unpublished, 2001).
2. Leigh Blackmore, J. Michael Blaxland, and Lindsay Walker, *Cathuria: The Newsletter of the Arcane Sciences Society and the Horror-Fantasy Society* 1, no. 1 (Newcastle, NSW: Blackmore/Blaxland/Walker, 1975): 1.

theme in Blackmore's poetry. Other unpublished work focuses upon topics and themes universal to the human condition.

Many of the poems selected are juvenilia, but it would be an astute reader who could identify them as such. Blackmore's command of the technical aspects of poetry writing, from a young age, is remarkable. The majority are technically faultless.

This collection is in two parts. Part I reflects Blackmore's interest in H. P. Lovecraft and his much imitated "Fungi from Yuggoth."[3] Like Lovecraft's "Fungi," Blackmore's "Spores from Sharnoth" might be considered a poem cycle rather than a poem sequence. That is, they are a collection of discrete works loosely connected in the weirdness of their subject matter; they are not a single work integrated by a story line, theme or continuity of time or place.

Both Lovecraft and Blackmore employ the sonnet, but Blackmore makes the form his own. The power of his rhythms drives the reader inexorably through his narratives to a denouement that bears all the hallmarks of terror—uncertainty, ambiguity and the readers' own uneasy imaginings! Blackmore creates a powerful tension through the certainty of his strong rhythms counter-pointing the terrible uncertainties of the content of his sonnets.

Part II reflects more diverse interests of and influences upon Blackmore. For instance, the influence of Clark Ashton Smith is evident in Blackmore's "Succubus" and his magnificent narrative poem, "Memoria: A Fragment from the Book of Wyvern." The concept and imagery of "Memoria" derive in part from Smith's "The Hashish-Eater."[4] Readers of Australian poets might also notice in "Memoria" images reminiscent of Kenneth Slessor. The apocalyptic imagery of "The Stars

---

3. In *The Ancient Track: The Complete Poetical Works of H. P. Lovecraft*, ed. S. T. Joshi (San Francisco: Night Shade Books, 2001), 64–79.
4. Clark Ashton Smith, *The Complete Poetry and Translations*, vol. 1: *The Abyss Triumphant*, ed. S. T. Joshi and David E. Schultz (New York: Hippocampus Press, 2008), 207–21.

Come Right" suggests some influence from Blackmore's early readings of Aleister Crowley.

In some respects Part I reflects the traditionalists' perspective of poetry with their emphasis upon traditional forms and sonority. Part II demonstrates modernist tendencies in form, cadence, subject and perspective. Haiku, free verse and song lyrics are included here. "Easy Money" shows experimentation by Blackmore and Ian Walker—they disassembled and recombined phrases they had written to create this poem. The subjects and perspectives of Part II poems are psychological and modern, rather than purely mystical and terrible. See, for example, "The Spiral Tower" and "Post-coitum Blues." "Pulp Jungle" is written in the idiom of late twentieth century popular culture, with its short sound bites, racing pace, and use of vernacular diction.

As a child of the mid twentieth century, Blackmore lived and was educated while debate raged about the value of old versus new poetry, and the new literary criticism. He did not choose between them—he practised both. The duality of style is not evidence of a progression from traditional to modern; it demonstrates Blackmore's virtuosity in the poetic form.

From European settlement in 1788, Australia's weird poetry has been scattered in anthologies of general verse, literary magazines and news periodicals such as the *Bulletin*;[5] scant collections of weird verse have been published. Much of the subject matter relies upon older European and American horror traditions with a smattering of local imagination, such as the mythological *bunyip* and the terror of the bush.

The title of Blackmore's "Terror Australis" is a word play on *Terra Australis*—The South Land—as Australia was known prior to European discovery. This poem resonates with antipodean fears and mysteries such as as pointing the bone, death in the desert and Aboriginal Dreaming. It

------

5. *The Bulletin* (Sydney: John Haynes, and others, 1880–2008).

has echoes of Dorothea Mackellar's much-loved poem, "My Country,"[6] in the contrasting images of European and Australian climate and custom. "Terror Australis" is a classic expression of Australian poetry in the weird vein. Others of Blackmore's poems meld international weird idiom and horror themes with subtle Australian influences of language, literature and the vigour of a still young culture in an ancient land.

Spores from Sharnoth and Other Madnesses has the rare distinction in Australian weird poetry of being published as a whole collection. P'rea Press is pleased and proud to commend Blackmore's surpassing weird poetry to the reader.

—P'REA PRESS

---

6. In *The Oxford Book of Australian Women's Verse,* ed. Susan Lever (Melbourne: Oxford Univ. Press, 1995), 59–60. See also online: http://www.dorotheamackellar.com.au/archive/mycountry.htm (for a copy of the poem, as at 5 May 2013).

ACKNOWLEDGEMENTS

To the spirits of H. P. Lovecraft and Clark Ashton Smith, whose yearning for vistas beyond human ken has always inspired mine; to Charles and Margaret Lovecraft, whose staunch friendship and extraordinary efforts in readying this little book for publication are much appreciated; to David E. Schultz for his interior design work, performed from a far land; to Gavin L. O'Keefe for his outré cover design and art; and to the indefatigable S. T. Joshi, than whom the weird and fantasy genres have no more knowledgeable apologist.

—LEIGH BLACKMORE

DARK DEDICATION

To whom the thrill of dreaming stirs the blood—
The pulse of nightmare quickening in the dark,
In scenes grotesque that flare and flow and flood
(Cold moon against the trees' bare branches, stark);

To whom the thought of dreaming thrills the soul,
Anticipation building towards the night—
Black fear of *things* that wing from pole to pole
And other Things that tremble at the sight;

To whom the dream is resonant with waking—
Grim grottoes full of shadows that are real
And silent groves that stretch the nerves to breaking
And gaping wounds that never seem to heal;

To whom their life is wan and sickly pale
Compared to those stark vistas of their dreams
Where crawling things creep on through storm and gale
'Neath dying blood-red planets, as it seems;

To whom unwelcome birth was thrust upon them;
To whom conception dealt a sickening fate;
To whom their fleshly raiments hang upon them
Like cerements of death, or rags of hate;

To whom their hard-fought struggle never-ending
Begs dark nepenthe, poured upon the soul
In ceaseless motion, whirling them and bending,
From suns supernal pressing to their goal;

To all those who pay homage to their vision,
Who long to dream and live but for the night—
Stand fast! And never fear the cool derision
Of those who *cannot* dream, who have no sight.

PART I

THE SPORES...

I

THE CONJURATION

In ebon skies more dense than dome or tower
Of dim Carcosa or dark Hali's deeps
(Where Hastur, though enchained, his vigil keeps),
There burns a star, lone symbol of the power
I call tonight. A cursèd, time-hoared work
It was wherein I found the pagan rite
By which to call the Thing, at dead of night,
From out the caverns where 'tis said to lurk.

I stand atop the hill and then—afar—
Discern a monstrous form that plants the seeds
Of madness in my mind, as swift it speeds
Across the void 'twixt Earth and white-hot star.
It grows in size, with such a speed as numbs
The brain. "My God!" I scream—"the Feaster comes!"

II

STARS RIGHT SOON

(with Charles Lovecraft)

With baleful fire, lit torches burned like stars;
The spindly trees thrust twisted arms aloft;
The Pole Star winked with evil light and soft
As comets streaked from Jupiter to Mars.
On this weird night men's souls were vilely spent,
And women lost their grip upon their minds.
Extinguished by a force that blackly binds,
The skies grew red, the roiling heavens rent.

The foliage whipped and trembled in the wind
As all assembled thrilled with pangs of fear.
A ceremony dark it was this year—
The sacrificial victim soon was pinned.
And in strange skies, a weirdly grinning moon
Seemed to convey the message—*stars right soon!*

III

Spores from Sharnoth

(with Charles Lovecraft)

The Spores from Sharnoth stir through endless night.
The dull dark void, as if black Fear itself
Shuns these dread seeds downpouring in their stealth—
Shows demon-things, contagious, spreading blight.
Like meteors they plunge upon the Earth,
Their colours iridescent 'neath the sky.
Unseen by any human eye, they lie
In wood and field, gravid with ghastly birth.

Black seeds of madness come from elder space
With latent life infested and imbued,
With alien life unthought-of, ill-construed—
Dark protozotes of weird exotic race
Flung forth by what mad god? A hideous jest,
These seeds of madness shall the worlds infest!

IV

THE TEMPLE

There stands upon a nameless Africk shore,
Amid the jungle's foetid overgrowth,
An antient temple—ruinous, and both
Deserted and forgotten by Man for
Countless aeons. Along the track once rid
By savage tribal chieftains and their kin
Lie shattered statues—not of brass, or tin—
But jet, and onyx, under stones half-hid.

Where merchant-monarchs brought their offerings
Of sandalwood and spices, herbs and talc,
Of fabulous gemstones and orichalc—
Now rubble lies, o'ershadowed by the wings
Of awful Time; yet lingers on an air
Of Something, crouched and waiting in its lair.

V

THE DARK GOD

A priest there was of that unholy fane
Whose crooked frame and old grey eyes bespoke
Knowledge of things before the world awoke—
Primordial horrors queer as he would fain
Have left unknown—but now he (like the din
Of waiting devotees without) is dead.
The rest are gone—and sooner would have fled
Had they full known what madness lay within.

The carven portals wreathed with weed and vine
Gape wide, revealing crumbled walls—and nigh,
Broken columns athwart the altar lie.
There, jungle beasts in strange obeisance whine
Before Tsathoggua's image, great eyes burn
With dark flame, knowing that He will return!

VI

THE DOOM THAT CAME TO SARNATH

I
(with Charles Lovecraft)

'Twas said the worshippers of Bokrug came
Down from the moon to build their city grey
Beside the vast still lake in Mnar. Some say
They called it Ib, though no man *heard* the name
Until a tribe of hardy shepherds old,
Uncounted ages later reached the place
And raised their city Sarnath; thence their race
Grew decadent, grew jealous and grew cold.

The men of Sarnath looked with fear and hate
Upon the beings of Ib. To kill their foe,
To overcome them, 'neath the moon's weird glow,
They plotted; cruel revenge they did await—
Pushed them, with spear-tips, in cold lake entombed!
The place thence called by men—*"Sarnath the Doomed!"*

VII

SARNATH THE MYSTERIOUS

II
(with Charles Lovecraft)

O! fabled Sarnath, girdled round with fame,
Renowned for gemstones—opals glinting fire!
City more aged than Babylon or Tyre
It stood old as the aeons when men came.
The walls of Sarnath endless things could tell—
And what ghoul-eaten things of slime and eld
Its primal-built colossal dwellings held—
Could they but speak, of deadly ancient spell!

Vengeance, by elder legend, brought to crave
Forbidden change to Sarnath's age-old ken;
The beings of Ib, deep-drowned by Sarnath's men,
Would wreak revenge beyond their watery grave!
Shadowed, like Cain's ill mark upon the world,
A *shape*—as of a monstrous wing—*unfurled!*

VIII

THE FEAST OF NARGIS-HEI

III
(with Charles Lovecraft)

Sarnath the Great ruled o'er the land of Mnar
When fast approached the thousandth yearly rite
Of Ib's destruction. Honouring the might
And pomp of Sarnath, men from near and far
Gathered within its marble walls to feast.
But silent hordes arose from out the lake—
Aquatic demons, devilish thirsts to slake—
And perished all the men, their revels ceased.

Those few who fled shrieked wildly of the horde
Of voiceless, green-hued, bulge-eyed things that burst
Into the gaudy banquet-hall accursed,
Presided o'er by one demonic lord.
The waters softly lap over the place
Where, once, Sarnath the Doomed had shown its face.

IX

PICKMAN'S MODELS

Half-human creatures gnaw on bone and meat;
Squat, slavering, and glaring with red eyes
From out the canvas. Things of fiendish size
And unconcealèd strength of limb, their heat
And stench fill senses all. Affrighted, seek
Beyond—behold the *child's* tortured face
Amidst the crouching blasphemies—the base
Of Richard Pickman's damnable technique.

Madness and talent, both in him are rife;
His brush a nightmare-spawning wand, Hell's fires
In pigment he sets down—yet never tires;
For Pickman paints his dreadful works *from life* . . .
Beneath the streets of Boston, loathsome beasts
Live over-nourished on appalling feasts!

X

THE NAMELESS CITY

The brooding desert gods watch o'er the place
Where silent, crumbling and accursed, it stands
Within a parched and terrible vale whose sands
Creep closer, although ne'er increasing pace.
What being hath seen its inner halls, long grooved
And lined with age? Or trod the stones that pave
Its dread (though empty) unlit ways? None save
The desert gods, unmoving and unmoved.

Its low, grey walls of grim, unvocal stone
(Hewn here in Araby, the land of Death),
Betray no hint of That which lies beneath,
Or shew that once a shocking deed was done.
Alhazred's *Necronomicon* says all—
". . . And things have learned to *walk* that ought to *crawl*"!

XI

THE OUTSIDER

The cobwebbed chambers filled me with unease;
Dismal stone passages I knew by rote
Stretched black, and silent; 'cross the putrid moat
Stood twilit groves of vine-encumbered trees.
I longed to leave the castle—so, at last,
O'ercame my fears and scaled the tower's wall,
Emerging on the earth *above* to crawl
From out the crypt—and through the dark—aghast.

When at the ballroom's lit doorframe I clutched,
The dancers screamed and fled (their revels spurned)
As from some grave-spawned fiend! I stumbled, turned,
And *saw* it then; threw up my arms but touched
The thing that brought the shock, which will not pass—
A cold, unyielding slab of polished glass!

XII

THE STATEMENT OF RANDOLPH CARTER

In through the oaks, just off the Gainesville Pike,
We turned, to reach the cemetery we sought;
And bore the lanterns, spades and 'phone we'd brought
Across the silent graveyard. Headstones, like
Fingers of titans dead thrust forth, leaned 'round
The slab where Warren found some hidden Sign.
We prised it up; he took one 'phone and line,
Left me one—and descended underground.

His voice came through the earpiece, faint and weak—
"If you could *see* this, Carter!" came a shout;
"God! *Curse* these hellish things—*legions!*—get out
While there's still time!"—his last scream reached a peak.
A silence followed . . . then, those words of dread
Which made me reel—"You *fool*, Warren is *DEAD!*"

XIII

Dream Landscape

None but the gibbous moon has ever known
The place in space and time of this drear scene,
Or what malefic dwellers may convene
Within its bounds. The pallid light-beams thrown
Half-limn empurpled canyons (petrified
And carved by stellar winds), which without sound
Tear wide the edges of the planet's wound
And shelter alien creatures, savage-eyed.

A stultifying lake fills half the plain,
O'erhung by deep and baleful fulgent skies;
Twin column-cinctured basalt cities rise
Upon the shore. Things, roused from their domain,
Flap noiselessly away from high-built walls,
Ope sharp-fanged mouths, and croak their weird death-calls.

XIV

UBBO-SATHLA

In steaming fens and mires of primal Earth,
The efts of terrene life are spawned and spread;
A formless mass bulks large on the swamp-bed,
The loathsome Source whence all are given birth.
Some, aeons later, take the form of man,
Oblivious to what they owe their mind—
An idiotic morass, star-born, blind—
And this, part only of the Great Ones' plan.

New England graves, the earth new-turned and fresh,
Lie in the rain as mourners walk away,
Turning their minds from thinking of decay:
The maggot now corrupts the stinking flesh.
Nor he who lives, nor rots, suspects—but learns—
To Ubbo-Sathla every life returns!

XV

THE SPHINX

The tombs of Aegypt's deathless ancient kings
Loom timeless and unhallowed from the sand.
Close by, the Sphinx stares out upon the land
Like that foul horror which Cassilda sings;
Or like that menace mentioned, in rune-writ
Tomes of black magic, with unnatural fear.
The weird half-man half-beast by many a seer
Was shunned—as cursed by daemons of the Pit.

The Black Pharaoh sensed its strange quality
Of latent life, and wizards vainly guessed
(Though none but Kephren long pursued the quest)
What huge and loathsome abnormality
Its stone was carven first to represent;
Some even now believe it *sentient!*

XVI

IN A SEQUESTERED CHURCHYARD WHERE ONCE LOVECRAFT WALKED

Dim past and present meld on College Hill.
Its houses brood, o'ertopped by verdant trees
Whose susurration fills me with unease;
Might gaslight's glow illume this place e'en still?
Here dreams the churchyard where vast elm trees grow.
One senses here the shades of writers passed;
One bows one's head in coming here at last,
Where Lovecraft's spectre pays *hommage* to Poe.

What honour walking where his footsteps fell,
Sensing with friends (and whisp'ring in hushed tones)
The spell of state-house dome, cathedral-bell,
Centuried ghosts amidst the hoary stones.
Mysterious truth this hidden churchyard gives—
In Providence today, Lovecraft yet lives!

XVII

PROVIDENCE: MARCH 15, 1937

Into the ward where, lying weak and still,
A pallid-featured man looks hollow-eyed
Upon the door, there comes with deathly stride
A silent, hooded figure. "If you will . . ."
Intones the spectre, taking Lovecraft's arm,
"It's time to seek what lies beyond this room."
The man gets up. "Surely you've come too soon?"
But, "Where to now?" he asks, his manner calm.

"Perchance you will," the visitor exclaims,
"Enter the realm of Chaos, vast and blind,
And groping through the gloom fatefully find
The aeon-old black book of daemons' names;
Will open it to see—mad truth of Hell—
In your own hand the letters: H P L!"

XVIII

RECALL

(For Charles Lovecraft)

It seems to me that I have lived before
'Midst ancient spires that chime with hellish beat—
Where gaunt and ghastly figures mix and meet,
And through queer elder volumes leaf and pore.
And I have walked alone (sometimes it seems)
Where alien voids and chilly star-winds blow,
Pursued by forms that move and dimly glow
Through darkling realms elusive as my dreams.

Uncertain scenes shift vaguely through my mind;
I'm beckoned by a call vast and remote—
Sonorous rhythms beating out a note—
Mysterious music, vague and ill-defined.
Past all that's earthly, with last memories strewed,
I realise *my own* infinitude!

PART II

...AND OTHER MADNESSES

INARTICULO MORTIS

He peers through hazy atmosphere
As through fogged glass or splintered door
Of derelict store to see pricked out by gaslight
Coarse dolls in faded dresses, taffeta and straw,
Crimped curls, cheeks daubed with paint,
On grimy shelves, their smiles cracked,
Relics of china, bone, hold out imploring arms.

Smeared mouths and ragged clothes entrance him,
Fix and thrall him as they crawl
With little weary movements through the dust.
His mind, befogged, gropes frightened to explain
The sun-bleached hair, the wide-mouthed grins,
Bodies that clumsy climb on pitted legs
And totter forward.

Pale faces chipped with age, hairlined with flaws,
Eyes fever-glittering, ink-circled and enraged;
Decaying yellow teeth bedded in spongy gums
Puffed out with poison. Terror grips him
As they push out past the doors of marble tombs
With stabbing jaws, grim treadmill pace.

They cannot live! His bulge-eyed gaze
Registers distended, rotting hulks
Of those who died long years ago.
But in their carrion grasp he *knows*—
As jerking figures choke out his life—
And he should know, *for he killed them.*

Post-coitum Blues

Through gardens full of floriated trees
And hedges stroll the two in thrall
To cruelly smiling Venus.
Her torch smokes and fills the air with sleepy light.
The tactile sense, he feels the colours run
Like swirls on carpet through a Cyclops' eye;
No further falsifying forms do furnish vanity
Or love in concentrated rosette form.
Tongues caged in mouths of silver-steel
Probe mercilessly; crescendo runs,
Satanic milk and thundersun,
Unconsidered temples, roots of seasonal change,
The insane laugh of chimera and boar,
Nickel-plated visions of Jesus
Build up the watchdog's muscle on waste.
The twilit hedges crouch expectantly
As shibboleth or ciphered calls
In his alcohol-eaten brain cells
Scream politely to snap it in two.
Miswatered by the landslide, she dreaming bares her breast,
Like floodtide's sacrifice or hawthorn tree,
To Fate who also stalks abroad this night.
When—bloody 'tween those crimson orbs descends the naked blade
And flowers a crimson wound,
Spatters the stucco honeycomb;
Pale fingers clutch in spasm, drop and leaden lie.
He lacerates the flesh to sculpt new life
From coagulum of carnage
Butchered murally in concord . . .
Discordantly the lingering peal dies.

MEMORIA: A FRAGMENT FROM THE BOOK OF WYVERN

I

Strong anodyne and opiate I quaff
To lull me slowly from the waking world;
The air hangs heavy, hot and drugged, as through
The mires of consciousness my sluggish mind
Sinks, ennui-swamped, to finally repose
Within the easeful lands beyond the Earth
Where often I have sought to calm my soul.
Lethargic movements cease and drowsy brain
Revives as glittering motes of dream-dust dance
Before me, coalesce to mirror thought,
And part, revealing lustrous marble walls
I knew before in lives long past. Behold
The city where aeons ago I dwelled,
And trained under the wizard's dark-eyed gaze
To reach the perfect peak of sorcery
In that forbidden quarter where alone
The seers and mages built their basalt towers
And cast their potent horoscopes and spells.
I enter through the giant brazen gates
And stand within the vast courtyard alone,
Where once the chimes of sapphire-spired fanes
Were sweetly heard and merchants from far lands
Displayed exotic wares to vanished crowds.
Around me, ornate balconies are joined
By stairs that spiral, ornamental walks
Whose balustrades and colonnades lead on
The eye to arches delicate and fine,
Resplendent domes and columned porticoes.

Tall, slender towers topped by minarets
Of coral rise from well-proportioned streets
Where polished statues of chalcedony
Stand gracefully amidst islets of green
Trim lawns, and fragrant gardens, zephyr-cooled,
Lie sleepy 'neath the sun's vermilion rays;
Proud peacocks spread their tails with shining eyes
Like purple jewels, strut regally past
Young trees in lovely orchards by the road.
Ripe, softly glowing fruits profusely hang
Among the drooping branches; on the air
Float scents of blossom-laden cherry boughs.
I move past silver fountains spraying still
Their light polychromatic water-jets
And leave behind the sector's opulence
To travel swiftly by well-known wide streets
Unto the onyx-paved sorcerer's realm.

II

In youth, I first espied the darkling manse
Where dwelled th' enchanter, he who reigned supreme,
And braved the dangers of its bounds to gain,
Through him, apprenticeship to evil gods;
Have dominion o'er all things natural
And occult by black art, and e'en command
That Source from which no man at last returns.
Beneath the carmine skies of this dread place,
I learned to raise the spirits of the dead
And take their secret knowledge unto me;
From rune-writ tomes of eldritch, antique lore
My mentor taught me all those formulae
By which man's brain, else feeble and infirm,
Can be borne up supernal 'gainst the plans
Of daemons baleful and maleficent
Which seek to overthrow magicians' power.
I conjured fiery angels and the rank

And file of Hell's hierarchy terrible;
Evoked (by rituals complex and reviled)
Great wheeling golden Phoenixes from out
The precincts of the sun; upon strange sands
I inscribed planet signs and summoned up
The lich who found the polished mirror bronze
Of sunken Poseidonis; I burned herbs
And incense from pure magic oils distilled
That necromantic servitors brought back
From Aegypt's shadowed tombs and temples dead;
And after years, did build an aedifice
Of porphyry and edomite within
The sorcerers' domain to take my own
Share of the treasures of the world without.

III

Now am I there once more at fall of night,
And as I gaze upon remembered things—
The blasting-wand and brazier, deviced
With lions winged and serpents venom-fanged—
Music by Winter's frosty wind-glance blown
Beats airy fists on mirror panes nearby
And I peer out to see the sunless globes
Of thick, dark night give way to clear, cold skies.
Light-rings, like blazing dragon-scalèd eyes,
Float there among the planets, each to each
Mist-dripping golden rain like running fire,
Deep-drowning hills whose snowy peaks uprise
From valleys rubbed like copper candlesticks
With moonshine; and ice-crystal clouds, illumed
By starry lanterns, snow the silent plain
With drifting flakes. Afar I hear a sound
Of footsteps manifold which nearer grows,
A muffled tread of iron gods below
And bronze monarchs striding past in the snow,
Making a file of sea-swept helmet plumes.

Their crusted garments flow beneath full beards
And faces leprous-white with dire portent;
They clasp great volumes, antient, vellum-bound,
And pentacles and rose-quartz chalices.
It is th' assembled might of all the town,
Combined for some reason arcane, who march,
Phantoms whose ivory staffs leave silver trails
On tilèd streets and gleaming ice-glazed roads
Unto the water's edge, and start to chant.
The rising song, the orison of power
And fearful malediction imminent,
Now strikes a chord in distant memory—
Was known to me, but lies beyond my reach.
The scarlet-streakèd sky pulsates with sound
Subliminal; a dull, low thudding beats
Upon my ears, assails my senses all.
Throbs, as of some unending heartbeat, move
The heavens (filled with amaranthine light)
To violent turmoil. Veils of crimson cloud
Tear wild across the blazing welkin; fires
Outpour the rift in opal-flashing streams
Of dazzling brilliance which transform the lands
Beneath, throw em'rald bolts on hill and vale,
Let flow prismatic floods on beryl seas,
Transmute the air to stained glass rare, and make
Aethereal gold o'erlie the moon's light side.
The iridescent landscape trembles, shakes;
The seas grow huge and hollow; massive waves
Of coruscating colours roar and pound
Upon the barren shore's wide sweep. The boom
Of surf and sky in unison with that
Arising from commanding sorcerers
Builds in intensity, cuts through the night
To hammer at the tower in which I stand.
The floor beneath me rocks; the giant panes
Begin to crack; the walls—rent stone from stone—

Gape wide and tumble; chill wind rushes in,
As does recall. I scream as knowledge comes
And I remember where I heard that chant—
The time I died before, as now I do,
Intruder in this realm. The world explodes.
Chill star-winds howl around me as I fall
Fear-frozen in the thunderous abyss
Whose gape rends wide the vacuum's fulgent stuff,
The spatial plane, and full reveals the glint
Of galaxies beyond our solar orb;
Star-shattered panorama of dead worlds
Where dust and rock alone behold the course
Of other planets, stricken, reeling down
The corridors of empty space remote,
To grind, and slow, and lifeless float; or flare
In brief vitality of death-throes huge
And inconceivable in scale and then
To drift away as primal cosmic dust . . .

ALONE

The dripping tallow,
Wail of child in distant dark . . .
The laughter of fear . . .

THE DEATH OF AUTUMN

The scattered petals
Pink and white, float winter-still
In scented water.

MOTHER AND CHILD

Full, soft and rounded
Fertility's primal form
Holds close her future.

OFFERINGS

Small birds from poets'
Finely-shaded pastels crawl
Into the steaming light.

ANTARCTIC VISTA

Towering bergs' cathedral spires
Float moon-engoldened,
Needle-tipped with icy fires.

ATU 0: THE FOOL

O Glyph of androgyne creative might!
O phallic Aleph breaking into Light!
Mad Messenger, who gambols in the dance,
Redeem the Grail, by bearing up the Lance.
O God of Silence, dancing 'neath the sky,
The influence of Kether, the Most High,
How subtly strange thy silent raptures break—
Harpocrates, as Parsifal you wake.

O Fool who art beginning without end,
Beware those jaws, the Negative transcend!
Ground of all things, primordial oneness sound;
O innocence, know Naught! O plough your ground!

O airy silent Babe in egg of blue
All wandering ways are lawful unto you!

Atu I: The Magician

O Beth, the House of silver Mercury!
The place where all imaginings can be!
Know thy True Self, create, absorb, divide,
Thine energies are triply multiplied!
The Wisdom, Will, and Word that make us whole,
Thou Messenger of Gods dost us cajole.
Deceit and Wisdom, with unconscious skill
Perform thy fateful juggling act of Will!

Thy Magick draws thy skills into one point
And summons all thy pow'rs—thy brow anoint
With holy oil; 'gainst dualistic fate,
True Will can various pow'rs consolidate!

O Father's Son, transmute the Logos ray,
Create the Word and Wisdom of thy Way!

To Clark Ashton Smith

O, Emperor of poetry sublime!
O, Bard of Auburn, seer of many things!
Thy pen has told with wit that sears and stings
Of shapes that lie within Poe's "wild, weird clime."
Your vision compassed dying stars and suns
That reel and totter down the aisles of space;
And with acerbic eye you viewed our race—
Its petty dreams your poetry outruns.

With golden pen you traced transcendent realms—
Vast worlds senescent, poisoned blossoms rife,
Exotic scenes of unfamiliar life.
Like ghostly ships with dead men at their helms
Your tales sail on, apocalyptic, old
Beyond the telling—veins of purest gold!

THE STARS COME RIGHT

(with Greg Smith)

Lightning splits a bible wall,
Through the dark life shadows creep—
Sieve the stem of mutant tissue call
Beyond the wall of sleep!

—Gerhardy Sachstein's *Flowers of Eschatus*

Within these hearts of wrath I mark
The doom of which the Arab wrote,
And death is sticky on the flower
Where lies the mangled goat.

Thunder clouds blacken every sky;
The Thousand Young are spawned once more;
The heaving seas throw up the Beast
Upon the poisoned shore.

The dawning age is burnt in flame;
The scarlet lips drip with decay;
A paling star sinks in the sea
Of bloody dew and fades away.

AFTERSHADOWS

By the waters of the Lethe on the farthest bank,
Where the drinkers crawl and the weeds grow rank,
Breathes a creature misshapen in the pale half-light;
When a drinker takes the bait, it will turn and bite—
Unwinking, unblinking,
With a face blanched and white—
Flyblown mirrors are its eyes . . .
A sullen mooncalf on its knees succumbs and dies.

Could this be the end? Could this be the end?

I'm sick at heart to think that we may never love again;
A thousand flickering memories, the visions we have seen,
The many faces we have worn, the places we have been,
The times that we have lived through—in frost, in hail, in rain.

Could this be the end? Could this be the end?

All along the Reeperbahn the lights grow dim,
And underneath the bridges swollen fishes swim.
Back into the labyrinth for a new Minotaur—
A fallen angel folds its wings and stumbles to the door.
Composure, exposure,
The slow drill starts to bore;
Something whispers through the trees,
A trace of coal-shaft misdemeanor on the breeze.

Could this be the end? Could this be the end?

The hewers of wood and the drawers of water
Weave dangerous nets 'round their sons and their daughters;
A sense of atonement lost in deep time
Lies buried, embracing the perilous slime.

Could this be the end? Could this be the end?

THE BIBLIOTAPH

In Acherontic caverns 'neath the earth,
Where stinking corpses line the ruined halls,
Where light fled not—but never came—the walls
Resound to gloomy cries of sullen mirth.

Colluvial bookshelves groan beneath black tomes—
Great volumes hasped with iron and with key,
All cobwebbed, filth-encrusted though they be,
Brought back to fill these mouldy catacombs.

Illimitably stretch the shelves of books—
Vile intermundane works darkly inscribed
With secret lore, with knowledge long proscribed
By all sane beings. Reaching with his hooks

Into their pages, frangible with time,
He soils them with his touch—his sole delight
To hoard these treasured volumes through the night
In this Augean domain a-crawl with grime.

He is the Bibliotaph; alone he dwells.
His pergameneous flesh hangs in thick folds;
He clasps a volume covered in thick moulds
Unto his breast, within these nether hells.

He grasps a volume that he cannot read—
Not read with *eyes*, but lo! somehow he knows
(His skin albescent, lolling in repose)—
What lies inside, what knowledge can be freed.

A famulus he once employed to feed
His mounting need; the servant soon was lost.
The Bibliotaph could never count the cost,
His knowledge useless as the urge to read.

He may be blind; the pleasures of his youth
Were squandered down the corridors of years.
He hears within these pages stained with tears
The fondled volumes whisper words of truth.

A life half-lived, in pages half un-read
Condemns the volumes breeding in his head.

To One Whose Name Is Yet Unknown

Upon some pinnacled and reachless peak
I dimly see you stand and start to speak,
A slender figure, lovely as the morn
Whose light is softly ushering the dawn.

I dimly see you stand and beckon me
From out the darkness; where I long to be
Is in your arms, my head upon your breast,
My lips upon your cheek, in careless rest;

All troubles, like great black and deadly birds,
Fled evermore away through your sweet words.
Your name to me is yet unknown but when
I learn it, there will be no sorrow then!

SUCCUBUS

Dead moons slumber in your eyes;
Pale and leprous is your face;
Parchment-like your withered thighs
That grip me in their dry embrace.

Harsh your fingers as they move;
Dry your breasts beneath my hands;
My doom is this convulsive love—
You scrape my skin, as desert sands.

I kiss your lips of chilly cold,
I clasp your crumbling, death-like form.
My mouth tastes full of bone and mould . . .
My mind surrenders to the Worm.

PULP JUNGLE

Strange stories fill my head,
Faces of fear and cries of dread (better stop thinking);
Ghouls are aghast they might be heard;
Extraordinary nightmares so absurd (might start sinking).

Throw away the book! Throw away the gun!
Drop everything and start to run!
Night visitors are creatures to shun!
Pulp jungle has lost its fun!

Supernatural powers desired,
Weird and wonderful dreams inspired (better stop drifting);
Scientific romance hot on my heels;
Telltale heart is how it feels (quicksands shifting).

Throw down the comic book! Throw away the knife!
Don't stop running, just run for your life!
Pulp jungle makes a terrible sound;
Haunted dusk is falling all around.

Scream and scream again for a ray of light;
In the pulp jungle it's black as night;
Fear itself has got me in its hold—
Pulp jungle gonna swallow me whole.

Homage to Arthur Machen: The Shining Pyramid

I

"Haunted, you said?" The deep and ancient wood
  Enshrouded Vaughan and Dyson, vague and vast;
  More mystic far than London evenings past
  The limestone-crested rim where now they stood.
  A vanished girl (the first of veilèd hints);
  Then signs appeared, suggestive of the rune—
  Strange lines, a pyramid, a crescent moon,
  Infernal almond eyes—composed of flints!

  Children, perhaps, at play had left their mark,
  Or gypsies with their secret signs of old?
  Dyson thought not—though dwarf, They must be bold,
  And what is more, They must see in the dark!
  "Unpleasant eyes," said Dyson—"Have you guessed
  What dreadful face those almond eyes suggest?"

II

Uncertain dread; a hushed and haunted air—
At length upon the wall are fourteen eyes!
Thence to the crag-line Pit; sibilant cries
Rise forth; at horrid forms the two men stare—
Like twisted children, forms that foully writhe—
The worm corruption, worm that dieth not!—
Like putrid offal, stirring through with rot—
Bound, in Their midst, a form once young and lithe.

A pyramid of fire gives ghastly birth,
Yet Dyson cautions Vaughan about the scream.
"To help her now, it would be just a dream . . .
That thing, she is no longer fit for Earth!
I fear, my friend, we'll never be the same;
I saw your eyes alight with inner flame!"

Easy Money

(with Ian Walker)

Tedious fingers beating on wood, this
Rain of coins upon this rock
Grinning with decay, wearily waiting,
Slowly unwinding, they mark.
> The coins continue to fall,
> The rain of coins goes on.
The nomad desperately punches at air
While night refuses to stay.
Discovered later: gold teeth in a corpse
Floating in the sandy bay.
> The coins continue to fall,
> The rain of coins goes on.

Terror Australis

I

The Southern Land—where snow but rarely falls—
In Yuletide brings the threat of searing fire;
Where sun and heat with sweat and dust conspire—
No holly and no ivy deck the halls.
The ground is shrouded here with naught but dust
And—scorched beneath the sun's incessant glare—
The sheep that dully raise their heads and stare
May die of thirst; the barbed-wire fences rust.

The celebration of the birth of Christ
Is shadowed here by legends dark and old;
The nights can be both comforting and cold;
The days string out like rope, knotted and spliced.
It is an alien land, where Christmas cheer
Gives way to trepidation and to fear.

II

A land of painted cabalistic signs
That lead us into pitiless vast space,
Where near and far and dark and light change place,
While jagged serpents dance along our spines.
Ghosts dwell here of an unrelenting kind,
Survivors of the famine and the flood,
Which rob men of their last remains of food—
Thrice-vicious ghosts that prey upon the mind.

A land whose secrets yield and break apart
To only those who live and die alone
(Perhaps condemned by pointing of the bone)
And see the truth at last in its dead heart.
Horrors half-glimpsed through waves of scorching light
Give way to freezing, arid, taunting night.

III

A Christmas here is not a Northern Yule—
Hot foetid winds defeat the gasping breath;
The arid sands give warning of stark death;
The ocean's roar portends a fate most cruel.
Did Lovecraft dream in "The Shadow out of Time"
A tenth of all the burning, torpid fear—
The horrors that inimical lie here—
In wait for dwellers in this alien clime?

Antipodean nightmares strange and bleak
Fill dreamers' minds with eerie visions dire,
That fill their souls with recondite desire
And draw them on to leer and shout and shriek.
Oppressed and tortured, baneful and malign,
With their grim fate Australians must entwine.

THE SPIRAL TOWER

I wandered in a wilderness of rooms;
I roamed the spiral tower up and down,
My eyes beset by inward-pressing glooms;
The spiral tower became th' entire town.

I wandered through the forest, city-bound;
I tossed and turned a-fevered on my bed,
My ears beset by wailing walls of sound;
The spiral tower closed in around my head.

My hand passed through the curtain of my flesh;
Stumbling and groping round distorted rooms,
I rose but fell, my wounds opened afresh;
The spiral tower told me of its dooms.

Trying to fly, I flap with broken wings;
I travel far but never reach my goal—
Bus terminals and broken, lonely things;
The spiral tower battens on my soul.

VALE OF THE VOLUPTUOUS: A PROSE POEM

I have dreamed long of a certain remote vale where the dark green boughs of luxuriant trees reach to the sky like lazily imploring sprites. Beneath the fronds of waving palms in the lustral breeze the dates grow thick with luscious fruit whose weight bears low the branches. Voluptuous and purple-lidded I saw thee there, reclining at length on a carven couch inlaid with porphyry and mother-of-pearl. A dozen dusky maidens from exotic climes, from Samarkand and Petra, fanned thee and dipped thy fingers in scented water and painted thy toenails with the red of flaming sunsets. O pale goddess, whose skin is as the milk of the hippogriff, whose hair is darkly lustrous as the deeps of night, thou who delightest me with thy smallest movement, whose raiment is the veil upon a thousand splendours—from the distant lands in my wanderings beyond the valleys thou knowest I have travelled night and day to find thee. Thou upholdest thy slender hand like a lily, and thy laugh is as silver strown upon the sands of an alien shore. In tranquil silence have I beheld thee at court with thy many suitors, seeing how thou dalliest with them but a little, but that thou then turnest them away and gaze with thy sea-green eyes into the distance, as though afar thou beheld a traveller in the desert. Then have I beheld there is a downcast to thine eyes and a sadness that the proud upholding of thy head cannot disguise. But see, I have brought thee grapes, rich and purple, from the lands to the North; and hangings, richly woven with thread-of-gold from the lands to the South. And I have brought thee heady wines that foam, from the lands to the East, and garments of finest silk from the lands to the West. Gifts from all quarters of this strange dim world have I brought thee. But these are only as trifles and trinkets, for a deathless love I bring thee also, and this comes not from the lands to North or South or East or West, but from the reachless depths of the heart. Dismiss thou thine handmaidens

and draw me with thy scarlet nails unto the white snows of thy bosom.
For there may I find surcease of sorrow, and thy sadness may depart, until
the guardian suns above shall fade to embers. And beneath their final
slumber we go down together unto the end of all things.

Ritual Invocation: Lvx/Nox

Let the dagger, chain and scourge
Banish all, but Spirit urge!
Let the dagger, scourge and chain
Banish all, but Soul remain!
Let the chain and scourge and knife
Banish death, and let in Life!

By the silver and the scarlet—
Let the gods produce a harlot!
Now the gods are in their session—
I abjure you, take possession!

By the bow and by the quiver—
By the ever-flowing river—
By the flashing eyes of fire—
Bring it through, my One Desire!

Though my face be nearly ashen
Still be present in your fashion;
Though my frame be torn and tender—
Though my Will be slim and slender—
Kindle all my Will together
Burning, burning, burning ever!

Slay the coward that would rescind!
Slay the part that says man sinned!
Perish cowardice in my brain!
Banish all—but Soul remain!

What shall we invoke tomorrow—
Tears of laughter, tears of sorrow?
By my magick might stupendous
Let the lightning rip and rend us!

INDEX OF TITLES

INDEX OF FIRST LINES

Bibliography of Poem Appearances

"Atu 0: The Fool." In *Spores from Sharnoth and Other Madnesses*, ed. Charles Lovecraft (Sydney: P'rea Press, 2008–). Rpt in *Sharnoth's Spores and Other Seeds*, ed. Charles Lovecraft (Calne, UK: Rainfall Books, 2010).

"Dark Dedication." Online in *The Specusphere*, November 2005. Can be heard online read by the author via: http://archive.org/details/ DarkDedicationByLeighBlackmore (at 5 May 2013). Rpt in *Spores from Sharnoth and Other Madnesses*, ed. Charles Lovecraft (Sydney: P'rea Press, 2008–). Rpt in *Sharnoth's Spores and Other Seeds*, ed. Charles Lovecraft (Calne, UK: Rainfall Books, 2010).

"Dream Landscape." In *Telmar: Magazine of the Macquarie University SF Association*, 1977. Rpt in *And Then I Woke Up!* Wollongong, NSW: Blackmore, Postill, and Wells, 2007. Rpt in *Spores from Sharnoth and Other Madnesses*, ed. Charles Lovecraft (Sydney: P'rea Press, 2008–). Rpt in *Sharnoth's Spores and Other Seeds*, ed. Charles Lovecraft (Calne, UK: Rainfall Books, 2010).

"Homage to Arthur Machen: The Shining Pyramid (I and II)." In *Terror Australis* 1, no. 1, Autumn 1988. Rpt in *Avallaunius: The Journal of the Arthur Machen Society*, no. 5, Spring 1990. Rpt in *Spores from Sharnoth and Other Madnesses*, ed. Charles Lovecraft (Sydney: P'rea Press, 2008–).

"In a Sequestered Churchyard Where Once Lovecraft Walked." Online in *Chaos Magic*, November 2005. Rpt in *Spores from Sharnoth and Other Madnesses*, ed. Charles Lovecraft (Sydney: P'rea Press, 2008–). Rpt in *Sharnoth's Spores and Other Seeds*, ed. Charles Lovecraft (Calne, UK: Rainfall Books, 2010).

"Memoria: A Fragment from the Book of Wyvern." Online in *The Eldritch Dark*, November 2005: http://www.eldritchdark.com/tributes/poetry/45/ memoria%3A-a-fragment-from-the-book-of-wyvern (at 5 May 2013). Rpt in *Spores from Sharnoth and Other Madnesses*, ed. Charles Lovecraft (Sydney: P'rea Press, 2008–). Rpt in *Avatars of Wizardry: Poetry Inspired by George Sterling's "A Wine of Wizardry" and Clark Ashton Smith's "The Hashish-Eater,"* ed. Charles Lovecraft (Sydney: P'rea Press, 2012–).

"Pickman's Models." In *The Arkham Sampler* (new series) 3, no. 4, 1986. Rpt in *Shoggoth*, no. 2, 1993. Rpt in *Spores from Sharnoth and Other Madnesses*, ed. Charles Lovecraft (Sydney: P'rea Press, 2008–). Rpt in *Sharnoth's Spores and Other Seeds*, ed. Charles Lovecraft (Calne, UK: Rainfall Books, 2010).

"Providence: March 15, 1937." In *The Arkham Sampler* (new series) 1, no. 4, 1984. Rpt in *Shoggoth*, no. 2, 1993. Rpt online in *Chaos Magic*, November 2005. Rpt in *Spores from Sharnoth and Other Madnesses*, ed. Charles Lovecraft (Sydney: P'rea Press, 2008–). Rpt in *Sharnoth's Spores and Other Seeds*, ed. Charles Lovecraft (Calne, UK: Rainfall Books, 2010).

"Pulp Jungle." In *Spores from Sharnoth and Other Madnesses*, ed. Charles Lovecraft (Sydney: P'rea Press, 2008–). Rpt in *Sharnoth's Spores and Other Seeds*, ed. Charles Lovecraft (Calne, UK: Rainfall Books, 2010).

"Recall." In *Studies in the Fantastic*, no. 1, Summer 2008. Rpt in *Spores from Sharnoth and Other Madnesses*, ed. Charles Lovecraft (Sydney: P'rea Press, 2008–). Rpt in *Sharnoth's Spores and Other Seeds*, ed. Charles Lovecraft (Calne, UK: Rainfall Books, 2010).

"Sarnath the Mysterious." In *Spores from Sharnoth and Other Madnesses*, ed. Charles Lovecraft (Sydney: P'rea Press, 2008–). Rpt in *Sharnoth's Spores and Other Seeds*, ed. Charles Lovecraft (Calne, UK: Rainfall Books, 2010).

"Spores From Sharnoth." In *Spores from Sharnoth and Other Madnesses*, ed. Charles Lovecraft (Sydney: P'rea Press, 2008–). Rpt in *Sharnoth's Spores and Other Seeds*, ed. Charles Lovecraft (Calne, UK: Rainfall Books, 2010).

"Stars Right Soon." In *Spores from Sharnoth and Other Madnesses*, ed. Charles Lovecraft (Sydney: P'rea Press, 2008–). Rpt in *Sharnoth's Spores and Other Seeds*, ed. Charles Lovecraft (Calne, UK: Rainfall Books, 2010).

"Succubus." In *Spores from Sharnoth and Other Madnesses*, ed. Charles Lovecraft (Sydney: P'rea Press, 2008–). Rpt in *Sharnoth's Spores and Other Seeds*, ed. Charles Lovecraft (Calne, UK: Rainfall Books, 2010).

"Terror Australis I, II, III." In *Spores from Sharnoth and Other Madnesses*, ed. Charles Lovecraft (Sydney: P'rea Press, 2008–). Rpt in *Dreams of Fear: Poetry of Terror and the Supernatural*, eds S. T. Joshi and Steven J. Mariconda (New York: Hippocampus Press, 2013).

"The Conjuration." In *The Arkham Sampler* (new series) 3, no. 4, 1986. Rpt in *Shoggoth*, no. 2, 1993. Rpt in *The New Lovecraft Collector*, no. 3, Summer 1993. Rpt in *Spores from Sharnoth and Other Madnesses*, ed. Charles Lovecraft (Sydney: P'rea Press, 2008–). Rpt in *Sharnoth's Spores and Other Seeds*, ed. Charles Lovecraft (Calne, UK: Rainfall Books, 2010).

"The Dark God." In *The Arkham Sampler* (new series) 3, no. 4, 1986. Rpt in *Shoggoth*, no. 2, 1993. Rpt in *Spores from Sharnoth and Other Madnesses*, ed. Charles Lovecraft (Sydney: P'rea Press, 2008–). Rpt in *Sharnoth's Spores and Other Seeds*, ed. Charles Lovecraft (Calne, UK: Rainfall Books, 2010).

"The Doom That Came to Sarnath." In *Spores from Sharnoth and Other Madnesses*, ed. Charles Lovecraft (Sydney: P'rea Press, 2008–). Rpt in *Sharnoth's Spores and Other Seeds*, ed. Charles Lovecraft (Calne, UK: Rainfall Books, 2010).

"The Feast of Nargis-Hei." In *Spores from Sharnoth and Other Madnesses*, ed. Charles Lovecraft (Sydney: P'rea Press, 2008–). Rpt in *Sharnoth's Spores and Other Seeds*, ed. Charles Lovecraft (Calne, UK: Rainfall Books, 2010).

"The Nameless City." In *Shoggoth*, no. 2, 1993. Rpt in *Spores from Sharnoth and Other Madnesses*, ed. Charles Lovecraft (Sydney: P'rea Press, 2008–). Rpt in *Sharnoth's Spores and Other Seeds*, ed. Charles Lovecraft (Calne, UK: Rainfall Books, 2010).

"The Outsider." In *The Arkham Sampler* (new series) 3, no. 4, 1986. Rpt in *Shoggoth*, no. 2, 1993. Rpt in *Spores from Sharnoth and Other Madnesses*, ed. Charles Lovecraft (Sydney: P'rea Press, 2008–). Rpt in *Sharnoth's Spores and Other Seeds*, ed. Charles Lovecraft (Calne, UK: Rainfall Books, 2010).

"The Sphinx." In *EOD* (*Esoteric Order of Dagon*), no. 5, December 1991. Rpt in *Spores from Sharnoth and Other Madnesses*, ed. Charles Lovecraft (Sydney: P'rea Press, 2008–). Rpt in *Sharnoth's Spores and Other Seeds*, ed. Charles Lovecraft (Calne, UK: Rainfall Books, 2010).

"The Spiral Tower." In *Spores from Sharnoth and Other Madnesses*, ed. Charles Lovecraft (Sydney: P'rea Press, 2008–). Rpt in *Sharnoth's Spores and Other Seeds*, ed. Charles Lovecraft (Calne, UK: Rainfall Books, 2010).

"The Stars Come Right." Online in *Chaos Magic*, December 2005. Rpt in *Spores from Sharnoth and Other Madnesses*, ed. Charles Lovecraft (Sydney: P'rea Press, 2008–).

"The Statement of Randolph Carter." In *The Arkham Sampler* (new series) 3, no. 4, 1986. Rpt in *Shoggoth*, no. 2, 1993. Rpt in *Spores from Sharnoth and Other Madnesses*, ed. Charles Lovecraft (Sydney: P'rea Press, 2008–). Rpt in *Sharnoth's Spores and Other Seeds*, ed. Charles Lovecraft (Calne, UK: Rainfall Books, 2010).

"The Temple." In *The Arkham Sampler* (new series) 3, no. 4, 1986. Rpt in *Shoggoth*, no. 2, 1993. Rpt in *Spores from Sharnoth and Other Madnesses*, ed. Charles Lovecraft (Sydney: P'rea Press, 2008–). Rpt in *Sharnoth's Spores and Other Seeds*, ed. Charles Lovecraft (Calne, UK: Rainfall Books, 2010).

"To Clark Ashton Smith." In *Spores from Sharnoth and Other Madnesses*, ed. Charles Lovecraft (Sydney: P'rea Press, 2008–). Rpt in *Sharnoth's Spores and Other Seeds*, ed. Charles Lovecraft (Calne, UK: Rainfall Books, 2010). Rpt in *Anno Klarkash-Ton* (forthcoming).

"To One Whose Name Is Yet Unknown." Online in *SFF World*, 2005: http://www.sffworld.com/community/poem/764.html (at 5 May 2013). Rpt in *Spores from Sharnoth and Other Madnesses*, ed. Charles Lovecraft (Sydney: P'rea Press, 2008–).

"Ubbo-Sathla." In *Telmar: Magazine of the Macquarie University SF Association*, 1977. Rpt in *Etchings and Odysseys*, no. 10, 1987. Rpt in *Shoggoth*, no. 2, 1993. Rpt online in *The Eldritch Dark*, January 2006: http://www.eldritchdark.com/tributes/poetry/34/ubbo-sathla (at 5 May 2013). Rpt in *Spores from Sharnoth and Other Madnesses*, ed. Charles Lovecraft (Sydney: P'rea Press, 2008–). Rpt in *Sharnoth's Spores and Other Seeds*, ed. Charles Lovecraft (Calne, UK: Rainfall Books, 2010). Rpt in *Anno Klarkash-Ton* (forthcoming).

"Vale of the Voluptuous: A Prose Poem." Online in *The Eldritch Dark*, October 2005: http://www.eldritchdark.com/tributes/prose-poetry-plays/2/vale-of-the-voluptuous (at 5 May 2013). Rpt in *Spores from Sharnoth and Other Madnesses*, ed. Charles Lovecraft (Sydney: P'rea Press, 2008–).

Spores from Sharnoth and Other Madnesses by Leigh Blackmore.
(September 2008; rev. rpt, August 2010, May 2013, February 2016)
ISBN: 978-0-9804625-2-4 (paperback) $14.50AU

OTHER PUBLICATIONS FROM P'REA PRESS

Richard L. Tierney: A Bibliographical Checklist by Charles Lovecraft.
(February 2008)
ISBN: 978-0-9804625-0-0 (paperback) $6AU

Emperors of Dreams: Some Notes on Weird Poetry by S. T. Joshi.
(November 2008)
ISBN: 978-0-9804625-3-1 (paperback) $14AU
ISBN: 978-0-9804625-4-8 (hardcover, out of print)

Savage Menace and Other Poems of Horror by Richard L. Tierney.
(April 2010)
ISBN: 978-0-9804625-5-5 (illustrated numbered hardbound) $30AU
ISBN: 978-0-9804625-6-2 (illustrated ebook) $10AU

The Land of Bad Dreams by Kyla Lee Ward.
(September 2011; rpt, February 2016)
ISBN: 978-0-9804625-7-9 (illustrated paperback) $14.50AU

Avatars of Wizardry by George Sterling, Clark Ashton Smith, et al.
(November 2012; rpt, February 2016)
ISBN: 978-0-9804625-8-6 (illustrated paperback) $14.50AU
ISBN: 978-0-9804625-9-3 (illustrated ebook) $10AU

Dark Energies by Ann K. Schwader.
(August 2015; rpt, August 2015; February 2016)
ISBN: 978-0-9943901-0-3 (illustrated hardcover) $26AU
ISBN: 978-0-9804625-1-7 (illustrated paperback) $14.50AU
ISBN: 978-0-9943901-1-0 (illustrated ebook) $10AU

Publishes weird and fantastic poetry and non-fiction
c/–34 Osborne Road, Lane Cove NSW Australia 2066
Website: www.preapress.com
Email: DannyL58@hotmail.com

P'REA PRESS